Dear Parent:
Your child's love of reading starts here!

Every child learns to read in a different way and at his or her own speed. You can help your young reader improve and become more confident by encouraging his or her own interests and abilities. You can also guide your child's spiritual development by reading stories with biblical values and Bible stories, like I Can Read! books published by Zonderkidz. From books your child reads with you to the first books he or she reads alone, there are I Can Read! books for every stage of reading:

SHARED READING
Basic language, word repetition, and whimsical illustrations, ideal for sharing with your emergent reader.

BEGINNING READING
Short sentences, familiar words, and simple concepts for children eager to read on their own.

READING WITH HELP
Engaging stories, longer sentences, and language play for developing readers.

READING ALONE
Complex plots, challenging vocabulary, and high-interest topics for the independent reader.

ADVANCED READING
Short paragraphs, chapters, and exciting themes for the perfect bridge to chapter books.

I Can Read! books have introduced children to the joy of reading since 1957. Featuring award-winning authors and illustrators and a fabulous cast of beloved characters, I Can Read! books set the standard for beginning readers.

A lifetime of discovery begins with the magical words "I Can Read!"

Visit www.icanread.com for information on enriching your child's reading experience.
Visit www.zonderkidz.com for more Zonderkidz I Can Read! titles.

*"Let your light shine before men, that they may
see your good deeds and praise your Father in heaven."*
—Matthew 5:16

Reader

ZONDERKIDZ

The Berenstain Bears® Play a Fair Game
Copyright © 2018 by Berenstain Publishing, Inc.
Illustrations © 2009 by Berenstain Publishing, Inc.

Requests for information should be addressed to:
Zonderkidz, 3900 Sparks Dr. SE, Grand Rapids, Michigan 49546

ISBN 978-0-310-76024-5

All Scripture quotations, unless otherwise indicated, are taken from The Holy Bible,
New International Version®, NIV®. Copyright © 1973, 1978, 1984, 2011 by Biblica, Inc.®
Used by permission of Zondervan. All rights reserved worldwide. www.Zondervan.
com. The "NIV" and "New International Version" are trademarks registered in
the United States Patent and Trademark Office by Biblica, Inc.® Zonderkidz is a
trademark of Zondervan.

Editor: Annette Bourland
Design: Cindy Davis

Printed in China

17 18 19 20 21 /DSC/ 19 18 17 16 15 14 13 12 11 10 9 8 7 6 5 4 3 2 1

I Can Read!

ZONDERkidz

BEGINNING **1** READING

The Berenstain Bears®
Play a Fair Game

**by Stan & Jan Berenstain
with Mike Berenstain**

Living Lights™
A Faith Story

ZONDERkidz

Brother and Sister Bear

loved all kinds of sports.

In the fall, they played soccer.

One fall day, Brother and Sister
dusted off their old soccer ball.
They ran to the soccer field.

Their team was called the Rockets.

They weren't the best,

but they were pretty good.

Papa Bear was their coach.

Their best players were

the Bruno twins, Bram and Bam.

Brother and Sister were good too.

Brother was best at corner kicks.

Sister could bop Brother's kicks

into the net with her head.

They didn't always win.

But it was fun just to play.

"Remember, team," Papa said.

"It's not if you win or lose.

It's how you play the game!"

There was one team

that only cared about winning.

They were called the Steamrollers.

Their coach said,

"It isn't how you play the game,

but if you win or lose!"

The Rockets' first game of the year
was with the Steamrollers.
"Do your best,"
Coach Papa told his team.

Mama and Honey sat in the stands.

Grizzly Gramps and Gran were there too.

Even their Sunday school teacher

Missus Ursula was there.

The Steamrollers looked huge!

So did Too-Tall Grizzly.

He was their best player.

Brother looked at Sister.

The Rockets were worried.

The referee started the game.

The Rockets had the ball.

They brought it down the field.

They passed the ball back and forth.

Bram headed for the goal.

"Take him out!" yelled

the Steamrollers' coach.

Too-Tall slide-tackled Bram.

"Foul!" yelled Coach Papa.

But the referee said,

"He was going for the ball.

No foul."

The Steamrollers scored a goal.

"How do you like that, shorty?"

Too-Tall said to Bram.

"That's enough!" said the referee.

"That is poor sportsmanship!"
said Coach Papa.
But the Steamrollers played rough.
At halftime, the score was
Steamrollers five; Rockets zero.

"You're playing a good,
clean game," said Papa.
"The Steamrollers don't play fair.
You don't want to win that way."

"It would be nice to score
a goal," said Bram.

"I know how!" said Brother.

"Let's set up a corner kick."

Brother put the ball in the corner.

He kicked hard.

Sister jumped up.

She knocked the ball into the goal.

But when Sister came down,

Too-Tall hit her hard.

"Are you okay?" asked Brother.

"I think so," said Sister.

The referee gave Too-Tall a red card.

He was out of the game.

The Steamrollers' coach

yelled at the referee.

26

Then Papa ran onto the field.

He started yelling too.

Soon everyone was upset.

Then Missus Ursula walked

onto the field.

"I'm very disappointed," she said.

"Is this how I taught you

to behave in Sunday school?"

"Remember," Missus Ursula said.

"Blessed are the peacemakers,

They will be called sons of God."

The coaches shook hands.

Everyone took their seats.

The game went on.

The teams played fair and had fun.

Steamrollers | Rocke

06 03

31

After the game, they all

had dinner at Burger Bear.

And they all felt like winners.